DANGEROUS
EGGS-PEDITION!

DANGEROUS
EGGS-PEDITION!

WRITTEN BY STEVE BEHLING

RANDOM HOUSE 🏠 NEW YORK

CONTENTS

CHARACTER PROFILES:

OWEN GRADY
Owen Grady is an animal behaviorist who comes to Jurassic World with his dog, Red. His job is to help transport dinosaurs to the new park.

RED
Red is Owen's dog. A very loyal four-legged friend, Red usually stays by Owen's side. He always wants to help and takes very good care of Owen.

MAX
Max is a scientist working on Isla Sorna, helping to prepare dinosaurs for their trip over to Jurassic World on Isla Nublar. She is very smart and has a good sense of humor.

HELICOPTER PILOT

The helicopter pilot who flies Owen to Isla Sorna is kind of a cranky guy. He's used to flying in a sky filled with *Pteranodons*, but that doesn't mean he has to like it!

THE ACU

The Asset Containment Unit guards make sure the dinosaurs stay where they are supposed to be and the Jurassic World visitors are safe.

"EXTRA-CAREFUL" DAN

A scientist who works with Max. Dan claims that people call him "Extra-Careful" Dan because he is, well, extra-careful. But he really isn't!

CHAPTER 1
SPECIAL CARGO

"You might want to hold on to something!" said the helicopter pilot. "Like, right now!"

Owen Grady did exactly as he was told, and held on tight to his dog, Red. The cargo helicopter veered to the left and right, back and forth, as a *Pteranodon* soared past.

"That's a *Pteranodon*!" Owen said. "They're amazing."

"They're a pain," the pilot said. "They fly all over Isla Sorna. Man, do they like the

helicopters. Makes landing here anything but easy!"

As the pilot steadied the helicopter, Owen looked out the window and down at some old, crumbling buildings on the ground below. "Is this where the dinosaurs were first cloned and raised before they were taken to the original Jurassic Park?" Owen asked.

"Yep," the pilot answered. "But once Jurassic Park's old owners left, they let all the dinosaurs loose to give them a better chance of surviving the big hurricane that hit the place. The island is full of dinosaurs now. Some are in containment units, and some are just roaming around. That is, until we take 'em over to Isla Nublar!"

Owen was an animal behaviorist. He really liked animals and was learning everything he could about dinosaurs so he could do a great job. He had been hired to help transport three dinosaurs to the new Jurassic World theme park on Isla Nublar. As the helicopter landed on a helipad, Owen thought about the *Baryonyx, Carnotaurus,* and *Stygimoloch* that he would be bringing back with him. He was so excited to see them up close!

As if sensing his excitement, Red sitting next to Owen began to bark.

"That's right, Red," Owen said, giving the dog a scratch behind the ears. "We're about to take a step into a whole new world."

"Just be careful *where* you step," the pilot advised as he powered down the helicopter. "There's dinosaur poop everywhere."

"Good to know!" Owen said as he and Red left the helicopter.

For a moment, Owen stood there, taking in the scene. The helicopter pad sat in the middle of a jungle clearing, with crumbling old buildings stretching into the distance. Judging by the fresh paint on the concrete helipad, it was the only new thing around here. Behind Owen, people were heading busily back and forth between the buildings, and he wondered who they were and what they were doing.

Remembering the pilot's advice, Owen kept his eyes on the ground as he moved on. He had barely taken three steps before he almost ran into a woman wearing a lab coat.

"Hi, I'm Max," the woman said with a smile. "Scientist. I work with the dinosaurs. And you are . . . ?"

"Owen Grady," he said. "Nice to meet you, Max."

"Owen Grady! The guy Mr. Masrani hired to transport the dinosaurs. You must be good if the owner of Jurassic World chose you personally! It's great to meet you, too," she said. Her eyes were immediately drawn to Red, and she blurted out, "You brought a dog here?!?"

"Well, Red's my best friend," Owen said. "He's always got my back. I don't go anywhere without him."

"He's awesome! Make sure you keep a close eye on Red, though," Max suggested. "The dinosaurs might take one look at him and think, 'Mmm, snack!'"

"Red's pretty smart," Owen said with a chuckle. "He'll stay ahead of them."

Owen looked down at Red, then heard a rustling sound coming from some nearby plants. He watched as a tiny dinosaur poked her head out, full of curiosity, and then walked over to him.

"Hey, that's a *Compsognathus*," Owen observed.

"That's right," Max confirmed. "I see you've been studying."

Owen nodded. "Little carnivores. And where there's one, there are usually more."

Almost as if on cue, another *Compsognathus* peered out from the plants, joining the first dinosaur in moving closer to Max, Owen, and Red.

Then came another.

And another.

AND ANOTHER AND ANOTHER AND ANOTHER AND ANOTHER!

"You have to stay alert on Isla Sorna," Max warned as she motioned for Owen and Red to back away slowly. "There's danger everywhere. And if you're not careful, it will come looking for you."

"I'll keep that in mind," Owen said.

"Pro tip," Max continued. "Do not try to pet or tease the *Compsognathuses.* I mean, ever!

Don't make any sudden moves, and they will eventually lose interest. Hopefully."

Owen nodded and watched as the *Compsognathuses* slowly wandered off. Then he and Red followed Max toward a utility vehicle.

Max reached into a side pocket on the vehicle and took out a tablet computer, handing it to Owen.

"You'll need to sign here for the *Baryonyx*, *Carnotaurus*, and *Stygimoloch*," she said, pointing to a box on the screen. "Once you do, they'll officially be in your care, and you can move them to Isla Nublar. According to Mr. Masrani, they're going to be part of a visionary, totally unique exhibit!"

Owen took the tablet and signed his name. Then he handed it back to Max.

"What do you know about these dinosaurs?" she asked.

"Well, I know that the *Stygimoloch* was a herbivore, and the *Baryonyx* and the *Carnotaurus* were carnivores," Owen began.

"*Are* carnivores," Max corrected.

"Right, right," Owen said. "Sometimes it's just hard to believe that dinosaurs really are alive again."

"Tell me about it," Max said. "I've been working here for a while now, and I *still* don't quite believe it! Now, let's give you a quick tour before you start the job."

Max jumped into the utility vehicle, and Owen and Red joined her. They drove a short distance from the helicopter landing pad toward one of the larger buildings Owen had seen on his way in.

"Welcome to the lab," Max said, stopping the vehicle. She jumped out and led Owen and Red inside the building. "This is where the science happens!"

Owen looked at a big room full of computers, with scientists huddled over them, typing away furiously. One scientist was wearing a bow tie and sipping water from a mug as he worked over an electric panel.

"Hey!" Max called out to the bow-tie guy. "Drinking water so close to the electrical controls isn't such a good idea."

"Don't worry," the bow-tie guy said, moving his mug away from the panel. "I'll be extra careful. That's why they call me 'Extra-Careful' Dan!"

Beyond "Extra-Careful" Dan, Owen noticed a series of glass-enclosed objects behind a plexiglass wall.

"What are those?" Owen asked.

"Incubators," Max said. "They provide a safe environment for dinosaur eggs until they hatch. Want a closer look?"

Before Owen could answer, Red ran over to the see-through wall.

"Whoa, Red," Max said. "You need to stay out here. Those incubators are very delicate, and we don't want you accidentally disturbing anything."

"I'll be right back, Red," Owen said as he gave the dog a pat. Red lay down and put his head on his paws.

Owen followed Max into the incubator room. He could see four large eggs being kept warm. "I recognize those from one of the books I've been studying. They're *Velociraptor* eggs!"

"That's right!" Max said as she turned to high-five Owen, who high-fived her right back. "And guess what? You're going to be taking them back with you to Isla Nublar!"

"I'm what?" Owen said. "I thought I was just taking *three* dinosaurs with me!"

"You are." Max chuckled. "*And* four dinosaur eggs. Mr. Masrani wants the eggs

to hatch right in Jurassic World. They'll be a big attraction for the tourists."

Owen felt a little uneasy about taking the eggs. They seemed really fragile. But he didn't have a chance to protest, as Max was already carefully removing the eggs from the incubator. She set each egg into an egg-shaped, insulated container and placed them inside Owen's backpack.

"These containers are shockproof, so they should keep the eggs safe during transport," Max said. "You know, unless something extraordinary happens."

Owen nodded as Max finished putting the eggs in the backpack. His attention was drawn to a group of *Velociraptors* in a nearby pen. The dinosaurs stared at Max, watching her every move. And now they were staring at Owen. He thought they looked upset.

"Those guys seem pretty interested in what you're doing," Owen said, pointing at the *Velociraptors.* "Should we be worried?"

"They're locked in their enclosure," Max said. "I mean, why would we need to worry?"

CHAPTER 2
LIGHTS OUT!

A few minutes later, Owen and Max left the lab and jumped back into the utility vehicle. Red ran alongside them as they set off. With the eggs safely in Owen's backpack, it was time for him to supervise the airlifting of the three dinosaurs back to Isla Nublar.

Approaching the helicopter landing pad, Owen saw the three dinosaurs, held in a massive metal cage. The *Baryonyx*, *Carnotaurus*, and *Stygimoloch* looked calm enough, as scientists and Asset Containment Unit guards prepared to raise them in the air with a huge crane powered by thick electric cables connected to the lab.

He and Max hopped out of the vehicle as they approached the dinosaurs.

"Is that helicopter going to be able to carry all three of them at the same time?" Owen asked, looking at the size of the creatures in their containment unit.

"Oh, it's carried more than that, trust me," Max said. "Everything should be just fine, as long as nothing goes wrong!"

An alarm suddenly blared out, startling everyone, as lights began to blink on and off all around the area.

"Aaaaaand something just went wrong," Max said, shaking her head.

"What happened?" Owen asked as Red began to bark.

"Power failure!" a scientist said, running in from the lab.

Owen noticed it was "Extra-Careful" Dan, who had been drinking the water. Dan's shirt was soaking wet.

"I think, ah, somebody spilled some, ah, something on the electrical control panel . . . maybe?" Dan said, looking *very* guilty. "So, *that's* a problem."

The workers on the helicopter pad ran toward the lab and the dinosaur pens, while the crane operator remained behind. Owen noticed that the ACU guards were running back to the lab as well.

"This is bad," Max said. "Without power, we could have system failures all over the island. Dinosaurs could break out of their containment units and pens!"

"So, what do we do?" Owen asked.

"Right now?" Max said. "You and I stay here and make sure nothing happens to these three dinosaurs and that they stay safe and caged."

A second later, the lights surrounding the helicopter pad went out completely, and the crane raising the dinosaur containment unit stopped working, too. The cage fell ten feet to the ground with a resounding CRASH!

The dinosaurs inside roared from the impact, which was so strong that the lock on their containment unit door opened.

"Hey!" Owen shouted. "ACU guys! We've got trouble!"

At once, some of the ACU team who had been running toward the lab turned around and ran back toward the helicopter pad.

The *Stygimoloch* seemed panicked by all the commotion and bolted through the now-open containment unit door. The *Carnotaurus* screeched loudly and poked her head outside the door just as the ACU arrived.

"Get that door closed!" cried Max, and a group of guards managed to shut the door. The heavy lock fell into place before the *Carnotaurus* or the *Baryonyx* could escape.

"We've got to get the *Stygimoloch* back!" Owen said.

"Don't worry, we're on it," one of the ACU guards said.

But Owen could see that the ACU was stretched pretty thin at the moment. Some of the guards were still struggling to keep the containment unit closed and the *Carnotaurus* and *Baryonyx* safely inside. And some of them were trying to make sure nothing else escaped from the lab.

By the time the ACU team was ready to go after the *Stygimoloch*, it might be impossible to find her.

Owen decided that he couldn't just wait around. Like Max had said earlier, he was the new guy. He really wanted to do a good job and prove to everyone that they had hired the right person. And since he was also a man of action, and even more of a run-headfirst-into-danger-without-a-fully-formed-plan-and-hope-that-everything-works-out kind of person, Owen figured there was no time like the present.

"C'mon, Red," Owen said with determination. "Let's bring that *Stygimoloch* back!"

CHAPTER 3
ON THE HUNT

"Hey!" Max shouted as she watched Owen jump into the utility vehicle.

He let out a loud whistle, and Red ran over, hopping into the seat next to him. Owen buckled his seat belt and fastened one around Red, too.

"Don't worry, I'll take good care of it," Owen said, patting the vehicle.

"I'm not worried about *that*," Max replied. "I'm worried about *you*! You're a newbie!"

Owen raised an eyebrow, looking at Max. "Newbie? I was hired as a professional animal behaviorist. Remember?"

"Well, it's true! But those are *dinosaurs,*" Max pressed, "and you literally just got here. This island is full of dinosaurs. Some are very *dangerous*! Do you have any idea what's out there?!?"

Owen thought about it for just a second.

"Nope," he answered. "But that never stopped me before!"

Max shook her head and reached into the back of the utility vehicle. She pulled out two walkie-talkies and handed one to Owen.

"Take this," she said. "At least I can keep in touch with you this way. You know, offer you some help when you need it? Make sure you're still alive?"

"Always a good thing!" Owen replied brightly. "I'll be back with that *Stygimoloch* in no time!"

Then Owen revved up the utility vehicle, hit the accelerator, and took off into the wilds of Isla Sorna. He was in such a hurry, he didn't even notice that he still had his backpack with him.

The backpack with the *Velociraptor* eggs inside.

* * *

"Grady, come in, Owen Grady," a voice crackled over the walkie-talkie. "This is Max. Are you there, Owen?"

Owen fumbled for the walkie-talkie and answered. "This is Owen. Hi, Max!" he said. "You're checking in on me already? I left, like, one minute ago!"

"Two minutes, thirty-five seconds, to be exact," Max said. "Anyway, I just wanted to make sure you were still—"

"Alive?" Owen said, completing her thought. "Yeah, I'm still here. Haven't been eaten by any dinosaurs yet."

"Of course you haven't," Max said. "I mean, if they *had* eaten you, we wouldn't be talking right now, would we? Anyway, that's not the only reason I'm contacting you. The ACU just informed me that the *Velociraptors* have escaped, too."

"Whoa," Owen said as the utility vehicle rumbled along the ground. He remembered studying *Velociraptors* and thought about what he had learned. He knew they were meat eaters—carnivores. They were quite clever, for dinosaurs, and they hunted in packs. Plus, they could run really fast.

"Thanks for the heads-up, Max," Owen finally said. "I'll keep my eyes open, but you don't need to worry about me. I'll be just fine. I mean, there's no reason that the *Velociraptors* would want to hunt me, right?"

Owen was so focused on the terrain ahead that he failed to see Red sniffing at his backpack. . . .

* * *

"Hang on, Red, the road's getting a little bumpy!" Owen said.

First of all, there was no "road." They were in the heart of the jungle, and Owen was driving along an uneven muddy path, weaving in and out of tall trees.

Second, to say it was "a little bumpy" was like saying that a *T. rex* was "a little dinosaur." The utility vehicle was bouncing around all over the place!

As Owen kept both hands glued to the steering wheel, trying to prevent the utility vehicle from crashing into a rock or a tree trunk, he heard Red barking.

"It's gonna be okay," Owen said. "But we have to keep moving if we want to catch that *Stygimoloch*."

Taking a moment to look at the ground ahead, Owen could see distinct marks in the mud. Based on what he had studied, he could tell they were *Stygimoloch* footprints. At

least Owen knew he was heading in the right direction.

But while he had his eye on the footprints, even for just a brief second, that meant Owen wasn't looking at the path in front of the utility vehicle, or the very large hole right in the middle of it.

The very large hole that Owen drove straight into!

WHUNK!

The utility vehicle's front wheels went down, and they rolled forward until the vehicle hit the edge of the big hole and came to an abrupt stop.

Luckily for Owen and Red, their seat belts kept them safely in place.

Unbuckling himself and Red, Owen climbed out of the utility vehicle.

"You all right, Red?" Owen asked, and the dog barked in reply. "Glad to hear it, buddy."

Owen looked around and saw that while the hole wasn't deep enough that he would need a rope to climb out of it, it *was* deep enough that the utility vehicle couldn't just drive out.

"Doesn't look like we're gonna be driving anywhere anytime soon," Owen said. "I'm afraid we have to follow those dino tracks on foot, Red."

The dog began barking once more, and Owen noticed he was focused on the area behind the front seat of their vehicle.

Before he could take a look to see what Red was barking at, Owen heard a rustling sound. He turned his head and saw a long, sleek head with glaring eyes pop out from behind some ferns.

"I think I just found one of the escaped *Velociraptors*," Owen said softly.

A couple of seconds later, another *Velociraptor* appeared next to the first one.

Then another.

And another.

"Make that all four escaped *Velociraptors.*"

The dinosaurs slowly emerged from the ferns, approaching the utility vehicle.

"Don't make any sudden moves, Red," Owen said quietly. "We need to get out of here, nice and slow."

Red barked back at him.

"Shhhhh," Owen said. "We don't wanna do anything that's going to make the *Velociraptors* angry."

The dinosaurs crept closer as Red continued to bark.

"You can't bark at the dinosaurs, Red!" Owen said, trying to get the dog to stop.

But Owen noticed that Red wasn't even looking at the *Velociraptors*. Red was barking at the area behind the driver's seat in the utility vehicle!

That's when Owen finally saw the backpack.

The backpack . . . containing the *Velociraptor* eggs!

"How did I forget about those?!?" Owen whispered.

CHAPTER 4
EGG ESCAPE

"Those *Velociraptors* seem really interested in those eggs," Owen said to Red in a hushed voice. "And Max said we're supposed to bring them back to Jurassic World! Let's take that backpack and leave quietly."

Owen reached into the utility vehicle, retrieving the backpack, as the four *Velociraptors* edged closer and closer.

Then Owen carefully stepped out of the hole, making sure to move as slowly as he could so he didn't upset the dinosaurs. Red followed behind him.

The whole time, Owen hadn't taken his eyes off the *Velociraptors*. They hadn't taken their eyes off him, either.

If Owen hadn't been so intent on watching the *Velociraptors*, he might have noticed that the hole he and Red had crashed into wasn't really so much a hole as . . . a footprint.

A very, very large footprint.

Backing away, one small step at a time, Owen saw the *Velociraptors* split up. Two of them approached him from one side of the hole, while the other two came from the opposite side.

"I know I said we should get out of here quietly, Red," Owen said. "But I think now might be a good time to—"

Just as the *Velociraptors* lunged for them, Owen shouted, "RUN!"

And like that, Owen and Red were off! They sprinted away, on two legs and four, as fast as they could go, the *Velociraptors* chasing after them.

"How fast can those things run?" Owen wondered. "Faster than us! Red, we might be in trouble."

But before the dinosaurs could catch him, Owen slipped in the mud and stumbled. He gasped when he saw that the flap on his backpack had opened . . . and three of the *Velociraptor* eggs had fallen out!

"Not good!" Owen shouted. "Not good at all! Whoa!"

As he slid in the mud, Owen started to tumble! He tried to grab the runaway eggs, but they were just out of reach, heading down the hill in front of him.

Red followed, trying to catch Owen.

Owen was worried that the eggs would break, but then he remembered that Max had placed them in separate containment units. He was relieved that they hadn't cracked!

"At least that's one good thing," Owen said. "I hope we survive this, too, Red!"

"Whoops!" Owen struggled to right himself as he watched the eggs continue to roll away. Glancing over his shoulder, he saw the four *Velociraptors* were still coming. But the dinosaurs seemed to be slowing, taking their time coming down the hill so they didn't lose their footing the way Owen had.

"That's something," Owen said. "Maybe I can use this to our advantage?"

Instead of trying to stop his fall, Owen leaned into it.

He was like a bowling ball, speeding down a lane—and the dinosaur eggs were the bowling pins!

As he careened down the hill behind the eggs, he saw a big rock rapidly approaching up ahead. The egg containers just managed to avoid smashing into it, but Owen wasn't so lucky. Throwing his body to one side, his foot caught the edge of the rock, sending Owen end over end as Red barked loudly in concern.

While Owen had avoided the danger of the big rock, he was now headed for an even larger one!

With the *Velociraptors* slowly picking up speed, peril seemed to be coming at Owen from all angles.

Watching as the eggs bounced and lurched around the larger rock, Owen tried to twist his body out of the way, but he was moving too fast. There was no way he would be able to avoid smashing into the big boulder . . . unless Red helped!

Sprinting ahead, Red chomped down on the back of Owen's shirt and pulled. The faithful dog yanked Owen aside, just enough to avoid the larger rock, but was forced to let go as Owen's momentum carried him onward.

"Thanks for the save, Red!" the mud-covered Owen said, slowing down. "I needed that!"

At last, Owen saw the slope of the ground beneath him begin to even out. He came to rest at the bottom of the hill and let out a long, deep sigh.

"I'm gonna feel that for the next five years," Owen said, every part of his body aching as Red bounded up to him.

Owen could still hear the *Velociraptors* coming down the hill. He blinked when he saw the three dinosaur eggs sitting in the mud right next to him!

"How's that for luck?" he said as he sat up and collected the eggs. He popped open the containment units and examined the eggs quickly. There were no signs of any cracks,

so Owen closed the containers and put them in his backpack.

The *Velociraptors* were almost at the bottom of the hill now, and they no longer seemed to be so cautious. They were flat-out running after Owen and Red, and especially after the backpack full of eggs!

"We're still in a tight spot, Red," Owen said. His eyes darted around, looking for some possible solution to their perilous predicament. To his right, there was a stand of very tall trees. There were lots of branches, which gave Owen an idea.

"Come on, Red!" Owen said, slinging the backpack over one shoulder. "We're going for a climb!"

Owen ran to one of the trees, with Red at his heels. Then he collected the dog under one arm and began to climb the tree.

The *Velociraptors* had arrived at the bottom of the hill, still seeming very interested in the eggs that Owen was carrying.

"Let's keep moving, Red!" Owen said as he continued to climb.

The dinosaurs were now at the base of the tree, and Owen could hear them clawing at the trunk. At that moment, a terrible thought occurred to him—what if *Velociraptors* could climb?

"That wouldn't be great!" Owen said out loud, answering his own question.

He heard snapping jaws as he scrambled even farther up the tree, before he and Red came to rest on a stubby branch.

Finally, Owen allowed himself to look down. A few yards beneath him, he saw the four *Velociraptors,* jaws snapping open and shut as they clawed at the tree, like they were trying to scramble up the bark but couldn't. After a few minutes, the dinosaurs seemed to grow bored and began to wander off slowly.

He and Red were safe!

"We did it!" Owen said, taking a deep breath. He was so happy, he started to laugh.

Which is exactly when the branch that Owen and Red were sitting on began to SNAP!

CHAPTER 5
CAMOUFLAGE CHAOS

"Hang on!" Owen yelled, and held fast to his dog. They dove from the branch at the precise moment that it snapped off the tree. Tucking in his legs, Owen curled up as he hit the ground, protecting himself and Red as they tumbled away. He thought about the eggs in the backpack and hoped the containers were still keeping them safe.

Behind them, the branch smacked into the ground. The rapid motion and sound startled the four *Velociraptors,* and the dinosaurs scattered.

Slightly dazed but mostly okay, Owen got to his feet.

"Ugh! That was unexpected," he said. "You all right, Red?"

Red barked right back, which either meant "Yes!" or "I'm really hungry—can we please eat now?" Either one of which was fine as far as Owen was concerned.

"Those *Velociraptors* have backed off for the moment," Owen observed. "So I think we need to get out of here, buddy."

Owen looked at Red, and the dog barked again. Then the two of them sprinted away into the jungle.

It took the dinosaurs a few seconds to realize what was happening. But when they did, they wasted no time in following. The *Velociraptors* unleashed a loud series of screeches as they tilted forward and chased after Owen and Red.

"And here they come!" Owen said, looking over his shoulder.

While Owen pondered the rapidly approaching dinosaurs, Red began to bark.

"Yeah, Red, I know, we're in trouble!" Owen replied.

But Red tugged at Owen's shirt, directing his attention at the ground.

"What's this?" Owen said, before he recognized familiar dinosaur footprints in the mud. "*Stygimoloch* tracks! Good job, Red! Follow the footprints!" Owen shouted, breathing hard. "And keep running as fast as you can!"

No matter how fast Owen and Red ran, no matter what they did, there seemed to be no way of losing their sharp-toothed pursuers. The *Velociraptors* just kept on coming, getting ever closer, and didn't seem to tire at all.

The same couldn't be said for Owen. He was *definitely* getting tired! He could hear Red panting heavily as well, and knew that his dog could use a rest. They had to find some way to catch a break.

As Red raced up a small rise in the jungle, sniffing out the *Stygimoloch* tracks, Owen trailed right behind. He stumbled, and to his surprise, a *Velociraptor* snapped at his leg!

"Yowch!" Owen shouted, pulling his leg away just in time to avoid a nasty bite. He scrambled over the top of the rise and slid down the hill, catching up to Red in seconds.

At the foot of the hill, Owen watched as Red followed the *Stygimoloch* tracks into a lush area full of leafy trees. Leaves were scattered all around the ground, too.

The cause for that was immediately apparent as Owen saw a herd of *Brachiosauruses* chomping on leaves from the tree branches. Eyes wide with wonder, Owen approached them.

"Wow! Look at these guys! They're amazing," Owen said as he and Red walked around one of the huge dinosaurs.

The sound of rustling leaves at the top of the hill drew Owen's attention. He looked out from behind the *Brachiosaurus* and saw a *Velociraptor* poke her head above the top of the rise. The three remaining *Velociraptors* appeared right next to her.

As Owen and Red hid behind the *Brachiosaurus,* Owen noticed that the herd of large herbivores had given the carnivores pause, because they didn't run down the hill right away. Owen had read about *Velociraptors* and how intelligent they were. They were probably sizing up the situation, making a new plan of attack as they tried to find Owen and the eggs.

"Then we need a plan, too," Owen said to himself. "And I think I have one."

He hurried over to Red, gathering an armful of fallen leaves along the way. Then, slowly, gently, he approached one of the towering *Brachiosauruses.* He had read that these dinosaurs were usually calm and preferred to graze and eat in packs rather than chase after people.

Taking the armful of leaves, Owen rubbed them against the *Brachiosaurus*'s massive, trunk-like legs. The creature didn't even notice! She just kept on eating her lunch.

Noticing that the *Velociraptors* were starting to descend toward them, Owen made sure that he and Red remained behind one of the *Brachiosauruses*.

Next, he dipped the leaves in mud and stuck a bunch of them onto Red. He put the remaining leaves on himself.

Red turned his head to look at Owen and whined quietly.

"I know, I know, it's weird," Owen said in a hushed voice. "But trust me, I also know what I'm doing!"

As soon as he said it, Owen thought, *I really hope I know what I'm doing.*

Owen slid down, until he was sitting on the ground next to Red.

In between the sounds of *Brachiosauruses* chomping on leaves, Owen could hear approaching footsteps.

"Stay still!" he whispered to Red.

A moment later, the four *Velociraptors* walked around the pack of *Brachiosauruses.* They drew nearer and nearer to the dinosaur that the mud-and-leaf-covered Owen and Red were hiding behind.

The *Velociraptors* didn't pay any attention to them! In fact, they walked right past the pair, sniffing the air. Eventually, they wandered off, heading into the jungle.

At last, Owen let out a long, deep sigh, and he could have sworn that Red did the same thing. "It worked!" he said. "By rubbing the leaves on the *Brachiosaurus,* we disguised our scent. All those *Velociraptors* could smell was stinky *Brachiosaurus*!"

From above, Owen heard the *Brachiosaurus* let out a loud moan.

"Sorry, no offense," Owen said.

CHAPTER 6
T. REX TROUBLE

"It looks like we've finally gotten rid of those *Velociraptors*," Owen said quietly, catching his breath. "Now all we have to do is follow the *Stygimoloch* tracks and lead our missing friend back to the helicopter pad. Piece of cake, right, Red?"

Red panted, and Owen thought he could see a smile on his friend's face.

Owen looked up at the *Brachiosaurus*, thankful for her help in hiding from the

Velociraptors. He gave the dinosaur a friendly pat on the leg. The dinosaur didn't seem to mind; she just kept on happily munching her leaves.

As he and Red were about to walk away, the walkie-talkie in Owen's backpack crackled to life.

"Owen! Come in, Owen!" said a voice.

It was Max!

Owen crouched behind the *Brachiosaurus*'s leg and dug into the backpack, grabbing the walkie-talkie as fast as he could.

"Max!" Owen said into the walkie-talkie, keeping his voice down. "Now's not a good time to talk! We just got rid of some hungry *Velociraptors!*"

Slowly, Owen leaned around the *Brachiosaurus.* His eyes were laser-focused on the *Velociraptors*, who were about fifty yards away. Owen thought for sure that the sound of the walkie-talkie would have drawn their attention. But, for now, the dinosaurs didn't seem to have noticed!

"Sorry, Owen," Max said apologetically, doing her best to speak quietly. "I thought you should know that the ACU are finally leaving on their mission."

"They just left now?!" Owen said in disbelief. "Shouldn't they have taken off a long time ago?"

"Absolutely," Max replied. "Let's just say they, uh, ran into a little decision-making problem."

"Then we're on our own, at least for the moment," Owen said. "Anyway, Red and I found *Stygimoloch* tracks, and we're on her

trail. Well, we *were* on her trail, until we got derailed by the *Velociraptors*. But they seem to be leaving now, so with any luck, we'll have the *Stygimoloch* back soon."

"That's great," Max said. "Keep me posted. Max out!"

Owen shoved the walkie-talkie into the backpack and sighed. He was relieved that the sounds hadn't caught the *Velociraptors'* attention.

It was time to get back on the trail of the *Stygimoloch*, so Owen and Red stepped out from behind the *Brachiosaurus*. In his haste, Owen didn't notice the twig beneath his right foot. And when he took a step forward, the twig went . . .

CRACK!

Owen couldn't believe how loud the noise was. It seemed to echo all around him!

Now *that* caught the *Velociraptors'* attention. Their heads perked up as they turned around with incredible speed.

At once, the dinosaurs glared right in Owen's direction!

"What?! Are you *kidding* me?" Owen said in disbelief. "Those guys don't hear the walkie-talkie, but they flip out over a broken twig?!?"

To make matters worse, the walkie-talkie crackled to life again just at that moment!

"Now's *really* not a good time, Max!" Owen said as he answered the call, starting to run away with Red as the *Velociraptors* sprinted after him.

"A quick update," Max said. "The ACU guards decided to split up into two squads. One group is chasing the *Velociraptors*. The other is going after the, uh, *T. rex*."

"Okay, first of all, the *Velociraptors* are chasing *me*!" Owen yelled frantically. "And second, now there's a *T. rex* on the loose, too?!?"

"Unfortunately, yes," Max answered. "Apparently when the power went down,

the *T. rex* escaped from her enclosure. And all the commotion on the island has drawn the *T. rex*'s attention. The ACU guards want to intercept her before she can cause any more trouble."

As Owen and Red ran, the leaves and mud they had covered themselves with fell away in a cloud. The *Velociraptors* raced through the cloud, screeching, jaws snapping.

"Hey, do I hear *Velociraptors*?" Max asked.

"Yes!" Owen shouted as he and Red emerged from some trees and into a beautiful green glade. "That's what I've been telling you! The *Velociraptors* are *here*! With *us*! And now you're saying that Red and I have to worry about a *T. rex*, too?!?"

"You don't have anything to worry about," Max replied. "I mean, except for maybe the

Velociraptors. Those sound like a problem. I'm sure the ACU has already found the *T. rex!*"

Looking over his shoulder, Owen noticed that the *Velociraptors* had abruptly come to a complete stop. They were no longer pursuing him and Red.

"Huh," Owen said. "Look at that. The *Velociraptors* stopped chasing us!"

"Oh, that's great!" Max said over the walkie-talkie.

Then Owen heard Red whimper.

"What's wrong?" he asked. Turning away from the *Velociraptors* to face Red, Owen finally saw the reason why the dog was whimpering and why the dinosaurs had stopped chasing them.

Standing on the opposite side of the glade, towering over them, was a terrifyingly large dinosaur that Owen couldn't help but recognize instantly.

"Max," Owen said calmly into the walkie-talkie as he froze in place. "Tell the ACU that I found the escaped *T. rex*."

CHAPTER 7
DINO STANDOFF

The *T. rex* took one look at Owen and let out an earsplitting ROAR.

Owen gulped, raising both hands outward in a calming gesture.

"Easy there, girl," Owen said as he and Red backed off. "We're just gonna go ahead and get out of your hair, okay? I mean, if you had hair. Which you don't. You might have had feathers, though, I think. When you were a baby."

Realizing that he was rambling, Owen stopped talking. For the moment at least, the *T. rex* didn't seem to be interested in attacking.

Save for a gentle breeze, there was silence . . . until Owen heard the screeching of the *Velociraptors* behind him!

Whipping his head around, he saw the four predators coming closer, claws bared.

"I think this is what they mean when they say 'caught between a rock and a hard place,'" Owen said to Red as he reached behind him, making sure the egg-filled backpack was still okay.

Red barked in agreement.

Owen took a second to assess the situation. It was not good. On one side were menacing *Velociraptors*, who Owen thought were either

after him or the eggs in his backpack. Maybe both. On the other side was an equally menacing *T. rex*.

"Any ideas, Red?" Owen asked. "Because I'm about out of 'em."

At last, the *Velociraptors* broke the standoff and came sprinting toward Owen.

"Duck!" Owen shouted as he threw himself to the ground, covering Red with his own body.

He was shocked when the *Velociraptors* ran past him! They now stood between him and the *T. rex*!

For a moment, it was like the dinosaurs had forgotten that Owen and Red were there. The mighty *T. rex* took a lumbering step forward, snarling at the *Velociraptors*. In response, the four predators screeched loudly and closed the distance between them and the massive dinosaur.

Owen wondered exactly why the *Velociraptors*, which had been so focused on catching him, were now standing between him and the *T. rex*. Then he realized what was going on.

"The eggs!" he said. "They're protecting us because of the *Velociraptor* eggs in my backpack!"

To an animal behaviorist like Owen, this was incredible. He was stunned to find that the dinosaurs would put themselves in such danger to protect their young.

"They're not so different from people," Owen said.

From behind, he watched the coming battle of the titans, as the *T. rex* and the four smaller predators continued to draw closer to one another.

One of the smaller *Velociraptors* had broken off from the pack and begun to circle the *T. rex*. If the huge dinosaur cared, she didn't show it. Her focus remained on the other three advancing *Velociraptors*.

"As much as I'd like to stick around and see what happens," Owen said, "I think now would be a great time to get out of here. What do you think, Red?"

Red barked in agreement.

Just as Owen and his dog were slinking away from the scene unnoticed, his walkie-talkie crackled again. "Owen?"

Owen practically jumped out of his skin when he heard Max's voice. He had forgotten he was holding the walkie-talkie!

"Max!" Owen said in a low voice as he and Red continued to sneak away across the glade. "What is it?"

"I was just calling to see how you were doing," Max said. "The last thing I heard was 'Tell the ACU I just found the missing *T. rex.*' I thought something exciting might have happened."

Owen chuckled. "I'll tell you all about it when I see you. Right now, the *T. rex* and the *Velociraptors* are facing off. I think Red and I might be able to escape and get back on the trail of the *Stygimoloch*!"

"Sounds good," Max said. "I'm tracking you on the GPS in your walkie-talkie, so I'll let the ACU know where you are—they'll be after the dinosaurs soon. And be careful. It looks like you're getting really close to a

ravine. There's a pretty steep drop there, so, you know, look out."

"I'm always paying attention," Owen said confidently. After all, he had managed to survive encounters with four *Velociraptors* and an angry *T. rex*. Surely a ravine couldn't pose a problem!

As Owen and Red got farther away, they could hear the sounds of the dinosaurs confronting one another—screeches and roars filled the air.

Owen was nearing the edge of the glade, with the dinosaurs about a hundred yards behind him. He was grateful that they hadn't noticed his disappearing act.

"All right, Max, I'll be in touch once we've got the *Stygimoloch*," Owen said. "Grady out."

"Awesome! Good luck!" Max replied. "Max out, also!"

"Things are finally looking up, Red," Owen said as he reached a stand of thick trees at the edge of the glade. "Let's cut through these and go after that *Stygimoloch*. I hope it won't take long to find her."

But as Owen pressed ahead, Red whined for a moment, digging his feet into the grass.

"C'mon, buddy, it's fine! The danger's back there!" Owen said, pointing toward the dinosaurs.

Owen smiled at his dog and pushed on through the trees. He took a giant step forward and immediately realized there was a problem.

There was no ground beneath his feet!

The trees at the edge of the glade hid the ravine that Max had mentioned—and Owen was now falling into it!

"Ahhhhhhhhh!" Owen shouted as Red jumped forward, catching Owen's shirt in his teeth. Red tried to pull Owen back, but his momentum was too great. Both Owen and Red were plummeting over the side of the ravine!

Twisting and turning his body, Owen managed to scrape against the rocky wall of the ravine. Throwing out a hand, he caught onto a stray branch sticking out from the cliff wall. Holding on tight, Owen then reached behind him with a free hand, grabbing Red tightly.

"That was close," Owen gasped, out of breath. "Remind me next time to be more careful."

Red barked. "I just did!" he seemed to be saying.

Owen and his dog were now dangling over the ravine, a raging river below them.

He shifted his weight as he tried to get a footing on the rock wall, desperate to climb up. But he slipped on some gravel, causing the backpack to slip off his shoulder and down onto his arm.

As it slipped, the flap opened, and one of the eggs fell out of the backpack! It landed on a ledge about a meter below Owen.

"Boy, this day just keeps getting better and better, doesn't it?" Owen moaned.

CHAPTER 8
HANGING BY A THREAD

"See if you can climb out of here, Red, and find something to help pull me out!" Owen said as he gently pushed Red above his shoulders with his free hand.

Red's paws found a foothold in the rocky wall, then some little cracks and divots large enough to help him scamper up the side of the ravine.

"Way to go! Good boy!" Owen said, proud of his dog.

Red barked from the top of the ravine, and then ran off in search of a rope, vines, anything that he could use to rescue Owen.

As Owen clung to the branch, his eyes drifted downward, until they came to rest on the egg sitting on the ledge below.

"I gotta get that egg," he said. "I think I can reach it, if I just . . . stretch my free arm. . . ."

And so Owen did exactly that, stretching his arm as far as he could. His hand grazed the egg. But he still couldn't quite reach it.

So he decided to shimmy his body, shifting his weight as he went a little farther out on the branch. His arm and shoulder were aching, and it was becoming difficult to hang on. But he had to do whatever he could to get that *Velociraptor* egg back!

"Come on," Owen said, stretching his free arm even more.

Finally, Owen snatched the egg! But in that moment, his other hand lost its grip on the branch, and he began to fall!

"Not good!" Owen shouted, protecting the egg in one hand, while trying to stop his fall with the other. He managed to snag a vine growing on the side of the rocky wall and held on as tight as he could.

No longer falling, Owen placed the egg into his backpack alongside the others as gently as possible.

"I hope Red comes back soon," Owen said. "I'd like to get out of here!"

While Owen waited for Red to return, he felt the vine slowly start to give. His weight was pulling it out from the rocks!

He slipped lower, now desperately clinging to the vine with both hands.

But the vine continued to sink down, and Owen along with it!

By this point, Owen was clutching the very end of the vine, watching helplessly as it continued to pull away from the rocks. Any second now, the vine would reach its end, and either snap or be pulled out completely. And Owen would fall into the river!

Just as things were looking their worst, Owen heard a rumbling from above. At first, he wondered if it was the *T. rex* and the *Velociraptors*. Maybe they had tired of their standoff, and had decided to come after Owen instead?

But it didn't sound like dinosaurs, Owen thought. No, it sounded more like a motor!

Wait, not just any motor . . . a motor*cycle*!

A moment later, the motorcycle engine turned off, and Owen heard a voice call out, "Owen! Are you okay? Hang in there, we'll pull you up!"

It was Max!

Then came the sound of barking, and Owen looked up. A moment later, a familiar face peeked out over the top of the ravine.

It was Red!

Max popped up next to Red, holding a rope in her hands.

"Red, help me lower this down to Owen!"

With an urgent bark, Red took hold of the rope with his mouth, while Max fed the other end down to Owen.

Not a second too soon, the rope arrived. Owen let go of the vine with his left hand and grabbed on to the rope. Before he could let go with his right hand, the vine snapped!

"Good timing!" Owen hollered as he snatched at the rope with his right hand, too. "Any later, and I'd be going for a swim right now!"

"Just hang on, and we'll pull you out of there!" Max said.

She began to pull on the rope, with Red anchoring the end of it. Slowly, they hoisted Owen up the ravine wall, inch by inch.

"That's it, Red. Easy does it," Max said encouragingly.

Red kept his teeth clenched on the rope and walked backward slowly, helping Max to hold Owen's weight and pull him out.

Things were looking good, when suddenly Owen called out, "Hey, Max! I think we've got a problem!"

"What? *Another* problem?" Max said. "How many problems are we gonna have today?"

"All of them!" Owen shouted. "The rope is fraying!"

Sure enough, the rope was coming apart in the middle!

"Pull faster, Red!" Max said as she felt the rope starting to give way.

The duo redoubled their efforts, yanking as hard as possible on the rope to bring Owen back to the top of the ravine.

But it wasn't enough.

The fraying rope broke, and Owen plummeted straight down, into the roaring river! He landed in the powerful current with a loud SPLASH!

"Owen!" Max shouted as she and Red looked over the edge of the ravine.

The seconds ticked by, until at last Owen's head poked out from the water downriver.

"A little help, please!" Owen shouted. At first, he tried to swim, but the current was

too strong. It carried him farther and farther
away.

"Come on, Red. Let's go!" Max said,
hopping back on the motorcycle and racing
away with the dog running beside her.

Down in the river, Owen saw several large
rocks ahead. He was moving so fast, and his
body was twisting around so much, that he

was afraid his backpack might slam against one of the rocks and the containment units might break, cracking the eggs!

After struggling to remove the backpack, Owen held it above the waterline. Passing the first rock, Owen switched the backpack from one hand to the other to prevent it from smashing into the rock. He repeated this action as he sailed past the next rock, and the next one.

Tired beyond belief, Owen wondered how long he could keep this up.

At last, he heard the familiar sound of the motorcycle again, as it came to a stop by the riverbank. Looking up, Owen saw Max, hands cupped around her mouth.

"Up ahead!" she shouted, then pointed toward the side of the river.

Owen's head sank under the water briefly, but he managed to resurface. He saw a river junction, where another, smaller river met up with this one. And there on the bank was Red!

Twisting and turning with all his might, Owen somehow made it to Red's side of the river, dodging rocks and saving the eggs all the way.

Just as he passed by Red, the dog again clamped his jaws onto the back of Owen's shirt and, with all his canine might, yanked Owen out of the raging river.

Max joined Red and helped pull Owen out of the water completely.

Resting on the bank of the river on his back, a soaking-wet, bone-tired Owen pointed at the pack on his chest.

Max reached in and took out the *Velociraptor* eggs.

"You did it!" Max said as she popped open each of the four containment units. "The eggs are safe!"

"Fantastic," Owen replied, falling backward on the ground, exhausted by his ordeal. "Can I have a short nap now . . . please?"

CHAPTER 9
STYGIMOLOCH SURPRISE

Owen closed his eyes for what felt like only a minute.

When he opened them again, he saw a shadow falling over him. Owen blinked, expecting to see Red. But something else was casting the shadow. . . .

It was the *Stygimoloch*!

"No way!" Owen shouted, waking up almost instantly. Sitting, he stared in disbelief at the *Stygimoloch* standing in front of him.

"You're awake!" Max said as she stepped out from behind the dinosaur.

Red barked playfully and ran over to Owen, licking his face.

"How long was I asleep?" Owen asked. "And how did you find the *Stygimoloch*?"

Max smiled. "You were only out for a couple of minutes. And we didn't find the

Stygimoloch so much as *she* found *us*!" she said. "Maybe it was all the noise of the rescue that got her attention. She just started nosing around and never left!"

Owen stood up and went to take a good look at the *Stygimoloch*.

"She's incredible," he said, wonderment in his voice.

"Most definitely," Max said. "And now that you're finally awake, we can get her back to the helicopter pad."

"Let's do it," Owen said, putting the backpack on. "But the first thing we should do is make sure our friend here doesn't run away."

Owen looked around to see if there was anything that might be useful to secure her. His eyes landed on some vines. And even though he hadn't had the best luck with vines recently, Owen thought maybe this time might be different.

So he tugged hard on the vines, breaking them away, then made a lasso at one end.

"What are you going to do?" Max asked

"I'm gonna rope that *Stygimoloch*," Owen said. "Just like a cow."

"A *Stygimoloch* is not a cow," Max retorted.

"Yeah, I know that," Owen said. "Still, I figure this ought to work."

Max shook her head. "Is that really a good idea?" she asked. "I'll go ahead and answer that question for you. No. No, it is not a good idea."

But Owen wasn't listening. He twirled the vine like a lasso over his head and, on the first try, snared the *Stygimoloch*'s tail!

"Bull's-eye!" Owen shouted as he pulled the vine tight around the dinosaur.

Unfortunately for Owen, this startled the *Stygimoloch*, which responded by running away at top speed.

"You're not getting away from me that easy!" Owen said as he held the vine tight, standing his ground.

Max shouted, "Maybe you should—"

Before Max could complete her sentence, Owen was whisked away by the *Stygimoloch*!

"—let go of that vine," Max finished. "C'mon, Red. The chase is on!"

Hopping back onto the motorcycle, Max put on her helmet as Red jumped up behind. She revved the engine and sped off after Owen, who was being pulled along the ground by the speeding *Stygimoloch*!

"Ow!" Owen yelled as his body was dragged across the bumpy ground. "I wish she'd slow down already!"

But the dinosaur was in no mood to go slower. She kept on running, not paying any attention to where she was going or what was happening to the man behind her.

"Owen, look out!"

Owen turned to the left and saw Max and Red coming up on the motorcycle.

"That tree! You're going to hit it!" Max warned.

Owen glanced forward and saw that the *Stygimoloch* had just swerved around an enormous tree. The dinosaur's sudden turn caused Owen to swing right into the path of the tree!

But then the dinosaur took another sharp turn, and Owen swung away in the opposite direction. He missed the tree by only a few inches!

"Whew," Owen sighed as he fought to hang on, making sure the backpack with the eggs didn't get smashed. "I don't need any more close shaves! And I've got to keep those eggs safe!"

"Don't let go!" Max shouted, steering the bike alongside Owen.

"Wait, weren't you just telling me I *should* let go?!" Owen shouted.

"Yes, but according to the GPS on my motorcycle, the *Stygimoloch* is running back to the helicopter pad!" Max yelled. "Whatever you're doing, Owen, keep doing it! It's working!"

"What I'm doing is hitting—*ow!*—rocks!" Owen gasped as the dinosaur dragged him over some big stones.

To Owen's relief, he could see the helicopter pad up ahead. The *Stygimoloch* was running right for it! He saw the ACU guards gathered there around two vehicles, standing by the *Baryonyx* and the *Carnotaurus*, still in their containment unit.

"Hey, look! Here comes the *Stygimoloch*!" one of the ACU guards cried.

Slinging a net across the pad, they gently caught the dinosaur as it ran through the middle of them, slowing it down, until it finally came to a full stop.

Owen was still holding the vine when the *Stygimoloch* shook its tail, freeing the vine and sending Owen flying across the helicopter pad!

"Oof!" Owen groaned as he rolled along the ground. He got to his feet just as Max and Red arrived on the motorcycle.

"I can't believe that worked!" Max said.

"Me neither," Owen replied.

He then checked the backpack to make sure the eggs were safe.

"Not a crack," Owen said, relieved.

From above, an approaching helicopter could be heard. Owen looked up to see the massive cargo vehicle hauling a containment unit with the captured *T. rex* inside!

"Wow," he said, taking in the sight. Then he asked one of the ACU guards, "How did you guys manage to bring her back?"

"Well, let's just say it wasn't easy," the ACU guard answered. "Basically, we tried everything except throwing a rope around her tail and leading her back here."

Owen laughed. "No, but seriously, how did you do it?" he asked. Owen was so curious about dinosaurs. He really wanted to know what it took to capture a *T. rex*.

The ACU guard grinned. "It took a lot of work, a lot of luck, and most of all, it took the *T. rex* deciding that she was tired of running around chasing *Velociraptors* she was never going to catch. When we showed up with lots of food in the containment unit, the *T. rex* ran right into it."

"Sometimes the simple approach works best," Max said, looking at Owen.

"Now all we have to do is round up those *Velociraptors*," the ACU guard said.

"Mind if I lend a hand?" Owen asked.

Max smiled. "Wouldn't have it any other way," she said.

CHAPTER 10
NETTING THE PRIZE

"There!" Max shouted as she steered the utility vehicle through the jungle. "I see them, straight ahead!"

Owen and Red sat next to Max, and the ACU guards followed them in their own vehicle. Max pointed to a stand of trees— just beyond them, Owen could make out the four *Velociraptors*.

"Now that we found them," Max began, "what's our plan to bring them in?"

Owen thought for a moment as Max brought the utility vehicle to a stop behind a rocky ridge, some distance away from the dinosaurs.

"When the *Velociraptors* were coming after me . . . you know, to get the eggs in my backpack? Well, then the *T. rex* showed up, and they pretty much forgot about me. All they wanted to do at that point was protect the eggs from the *T. rex*," Owen said.

Max nodded, her eyes widening. She smiled and grabbed Owen's shoulders, shaking him.

"You've just given me an amazing idea!" she said, making sure not to disturb the dinosaurs. "Oh, I love it! But you may not like it. . . ."

* * *

"Hey, Max! Remember when you said I may not like it?" Owen asked as he dangled from a rope hanging from the top of the rocky ridge, the backpack of eggs slung over his shoulders.

"Yep!" Max said, keeping an eye on the *Velociraptors* from the ground below.

"Well, you were right," Owen answered. "Tell me, why does this plan require me to be hanging from a cliff?"

He *really* wasn't thrilled about hanging from a cliff again. And he was even *less* thrilled about the part that was coming next.

"If the plan is going to work, we need you to look as helpless as possible!" Max answered.

Above him, Owen watched as a *Pteranodon* soared through the air, circling him.

Except it wasn't really a *Pteranodon*. It was a hastily built yet surprisingly convincing puppet, made from sticks, rope, mud, leaves, grass, and whatever Max and Owen had been able to find. A couple of ACU guards sat in some bushes atop the ridge, and with tree branches and rope tied to the puppet, they made it seem like the *Pteranodon* was flying.

Max hoped that their ruse would seem real enough to the *Velociraptors*, so when the flying creature looked to be endangering the eggs in Owen's backpack, they would come running.

"All right, Owen. Get ready!" Max said, glancing back and forth between him and the four dinosaurs. "Wait for it! Aaaand . . . action!"

"Help!" Owen shouted as loudly as he could, looking over his shoulder at his backpack. "That . . . thing that's clearly a *Pteranodon* and not a puppet is going to eat these *Velociraptor* eggs!"

The sound of Owen's desperate scream of "Help!" got the dinosaurs' attention, and they looked up. Their eyes narrowed as they saw Owen—and smelled the eggs stored in his backpack, which they clearly remembered. Screeching loudly, the *Velociraptors* crouched down low.

Then they ran, heading toward the steep incline behind Max that led to the top of the ridge.

"It's working!" Max said excitedly. "They're going to take out the *Pteranodon* to save the eggs!"

The *Velociraptors* sprinted toward Max, quickly closing the distance. They were so intent on saving the backpack of eggs, they didn't notice a large patch of sand between them and Max.

"Careful, Max!" Owen yelled.

"I got it! Don't worry!" Max replied.

As soon as the four *Velociraptors* ran across the sand, Max tugged hard on a hidden rope. She was joined by three ACU guards, who pulled on three more ropes.

At once, the dinosaurs were caught in a huge net that had been hidden under the sand!

The *Velociraptors* screeched in protest, but they couldn't escape the net.

"We did it, guys!" Max said, jumping up and down.

"Great work, everyone!" Owen said, hanging from the rope. "Now, can someone get me down?"

* * *

After Owen had been "rescued" and a cargo helicopter took the *Velociraptors* back to their pen, everyone returned to the helicopter pad.

"Well, *this* was a fun day!" Max said to Owen with a smile as they rested in the utility vehicle.

Owen laughed. "Not too bad," he said. "Got a lot done. Caught a *Stygimoloch*, faced off against a *T. rex*, helped return some *Velociraptors* to their home, and saved a handful of dinosaur eggs!"

"One thing's for sure," Max said. "You're no longer a newbie!"

"Thanks, Max," Owen said. "I really appreciate that."

As they watched the ACU guards take the *Velociraptors* back to their pen, Owen smiled.

"They're pretty amazing," he observed. "I can't get over the way they moved to protect those eggs."

"I wonder if it was only that," Max said, looking at Owen. "If they had really wanted to, those *Velociraptors* could have taken you down *and* protected the eggs—but they didn't harm you. Let's just say that I'm super impressed!"

"Thanks," Owen said. "I wish I could spend more time with them."

"Well, I'll be taking good care of these guys," Max said as she pointed at the four dinosaurs. "They're going to stay here on

Isla Sorna. If you decide to stick around, come by and hang out with us!"

"I'd like that!" Owen said with a smile.

"Take good care of those eggs," Max said. "Who knows? Maybe when they hatch, they'll recognize you!"

"Wouldn't that be something," Owen said. He wondered if it would be possible to train a *Velociraptor,* the way he had trained Red.

Just then, the helicopter pilot ran over to Owen and Max.

"Mr. Grady?" the pilot said. "We're ready for you. It's time to get the *Baryonyx, Carnotaurus,* and *Stygimoloch* over to Isla Nublar. And those eggs!"

Max walked Owen and Red to the cargo helicopter. "See you around Jurassic World," Max said.

"Who knows," Owen replied. "You just might!"

Then he and Red hopped into the helicopter before it rose into the air.

Owen waved through the window and watched the figure of Max grow smaller and smaller as the helicopter flew away.

A minute later, Isla Sorna was already behind them.

"Some bad weather rolling in," came a static-filled voice from the helicopter's radio. "Real bad!"

"Looks like I'll be asking you to hold on to something again," the pilot said.

"That's okay," Owen replied with a grin, as Red woofed. "I'm getting used to it!"

VELOCIRAPTOR

Carnivorous dinosaur, with long claws and sharp teeth. Very fast and agile, hunts in packs. It is advised to take extra care during an encounter.

I still feel shivers running down my spine when I remember my first meeting with them, even though I'm a gutsy guy!

SIZE:	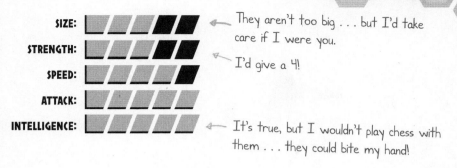
STRENGTH:	
SPEED:	
ATTACK:	
INTELLIGENCE:	

They aren't too big . . . but I'd take care if I were you.

I'd give a 4!

It's true, but I wouldn't play chess with them . . . they could bite my hand!

ONTAINMENT:

angerous species. Needs to be kept in a compound containing stretches of grassy plain and ccess to water, e.g., a small lake.

The main problem is that they can find their way out really quickly!

HARACTERISTICS:

lever and cunning predator. Individual animals work together during a hunt.

nd they are sooo good at it! I met them for the first time during the adventure with he eggs, and I barely made it out alive! But I'm one tough cookie, and I hung in there.

PERATIONAL COMMENTS:

ery interesting animals. It is suggested to continue observation and attempts at training.

Apart from being a gutsy guy, I'm also an animal behaviorist and a training specialist. Training raptors can be a real challenge, but "Owen Grady, raptor trainer" sounds pretty cool . . . I need to think about it!